MARVEL

THE INVINCIBLE™ IRON MAN VS = THE = MANDARIN™

Based on the Marvel comic book series
The Invincible Iron Man
Adapted by Tomas Palacios
Cover Illustrated by Mike Norton
and Brian Miller
Interior Illustrated by Craig Rousseau
and Hi-Fi Design

Published by Marvel Press, an imprint of Disney Book Group. No part of this book may be reproduced or transmitted in any form or by any means, electronic or mechanical, including photocopying, recording, or by any information storage and retrieval system, without written permission from the publisher.

For information address Marvel Press, 114 Fifth Avenue, New York, New York 10011-5690.
Printed in the United States of America
First Edition
1 3 5 7 9 10 8 6 4 2
G658-7729-4-12289
ISBN 978-1-4231-4289-8

TM & © 2012 Marvel & Subs.
marvelkids.com

MARVEL
New York

SUSTAINABLE FORESTRY INITIATIVE
Certified Chain of Custody
Promoting Sustainable Forestry
www.sfiprogram.org
SFI-01415
The SFI label applies to the text stock

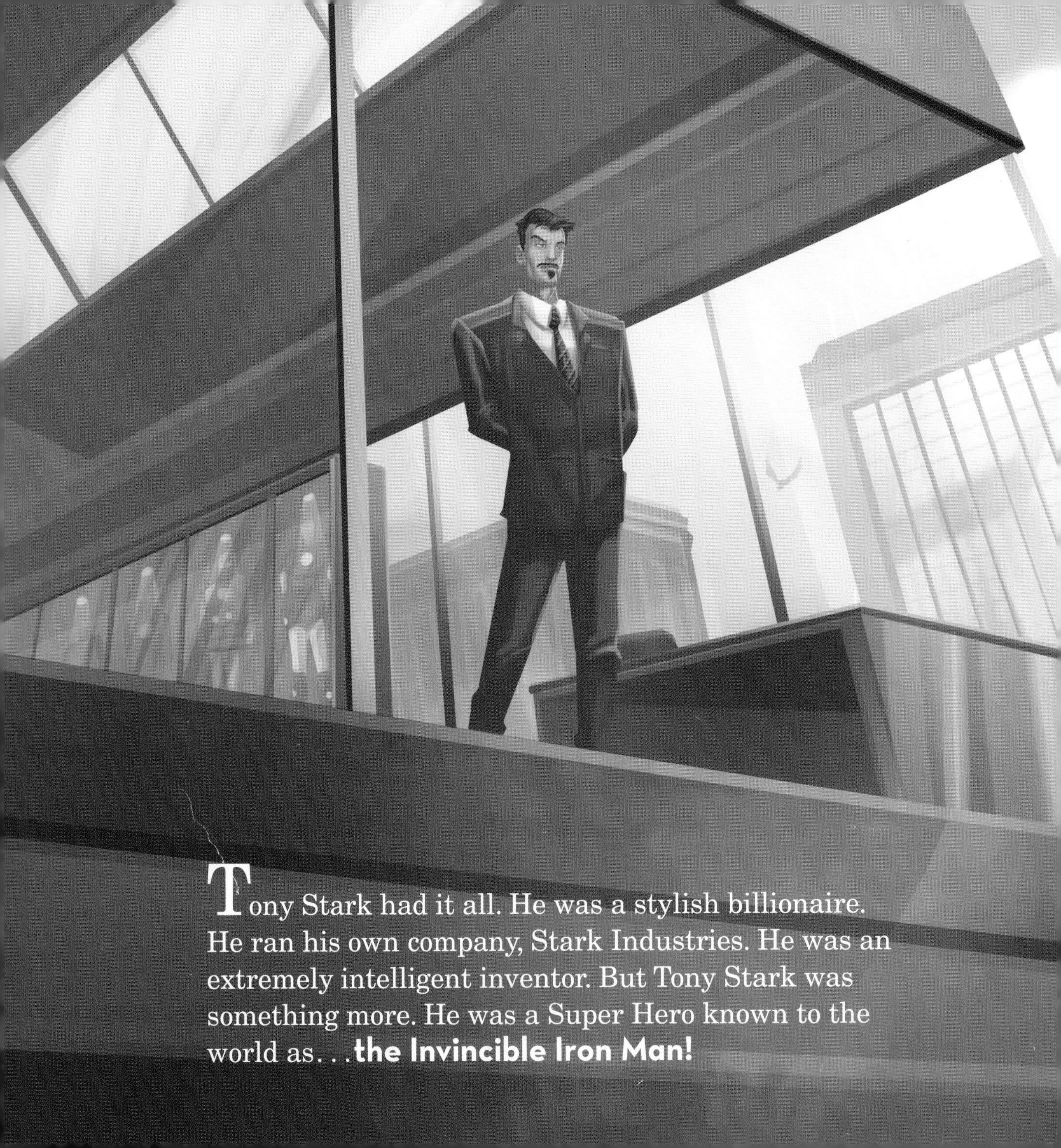

Tony Stark had it all. He was a stylish billionaire. He ran his own company, Stark Industries. He was an extremely intelligent inventor. But Tony Stark was something more. He was a Super Hero known to the world as. . . **the Invincible Iron Man!**

A story on the news caught Tony's attention.

"In Southeast Asia, the superpowered villain known only as the Mandarin has struck again, stealing several crates of US technology belonging to billionaire inventor **Tony Stark,"** said the reporter. "Just last week, the Mandarin attacked a local village, claiming to be the new ruler of their land. . . ."

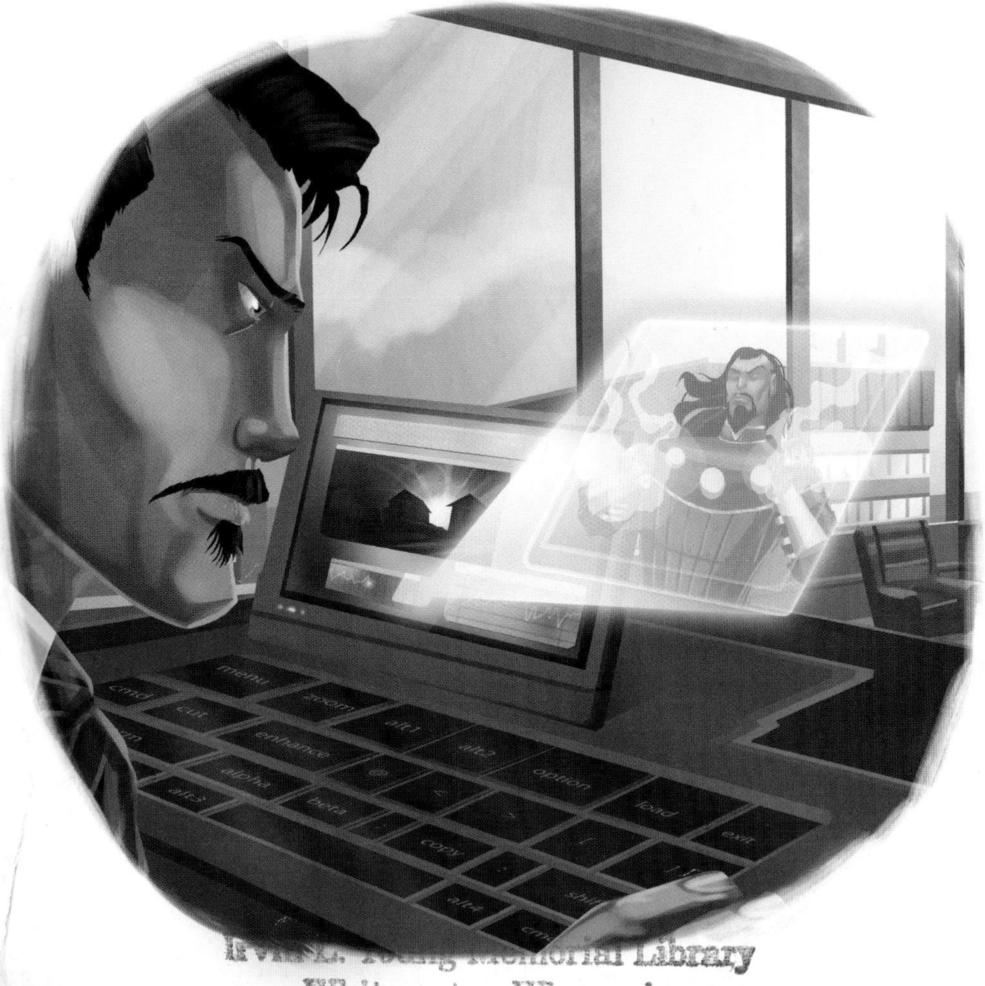
menu
cmd
cut
zoom
enhance
option
alpha
beta
load
exit
copy

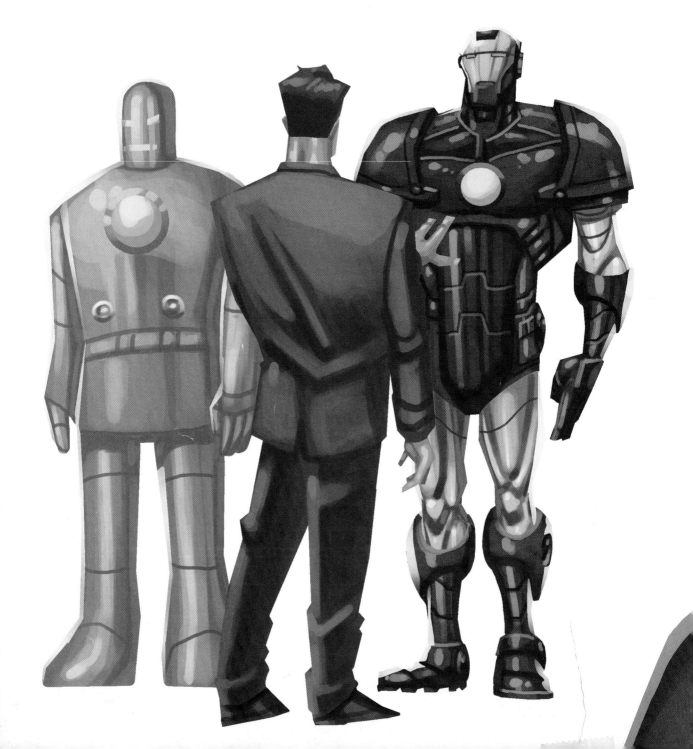

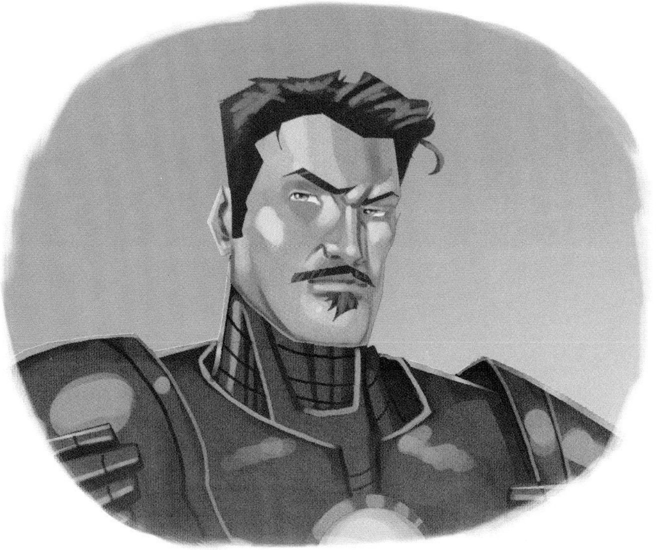

Tony stepped into his armor.

"This calls for a **man made of iron. . . .**"

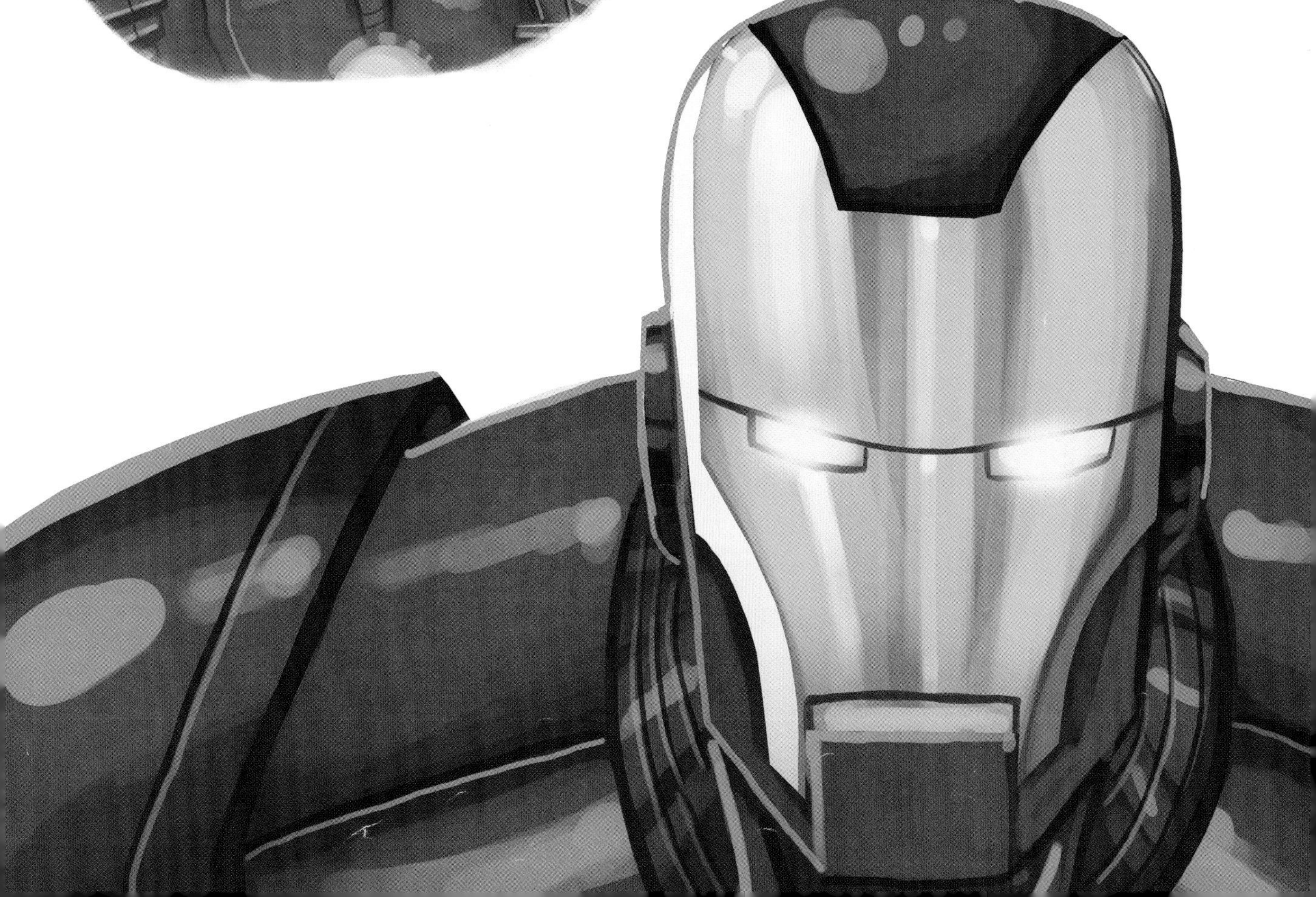

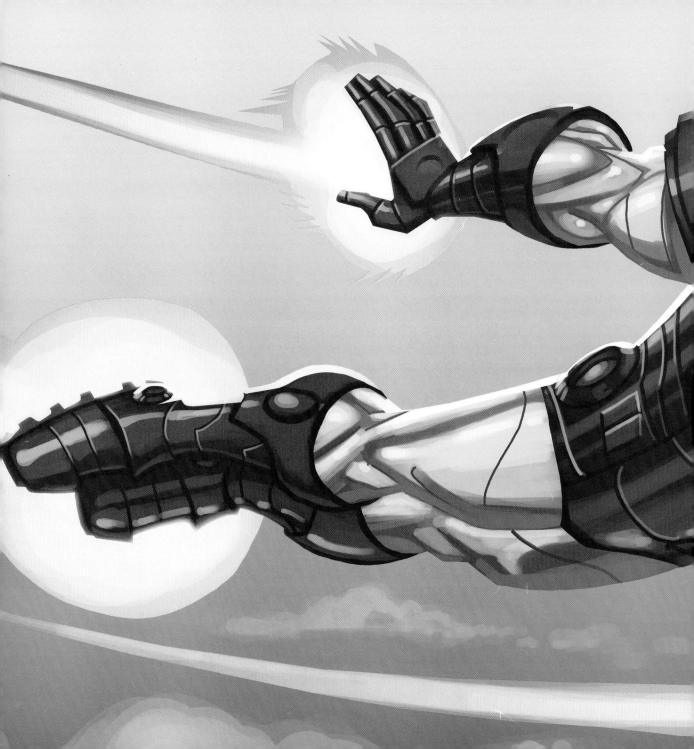

The Invincible Iron Man blasted across the sunny sky.

At this rate, I’ll reach the Far East in no time! Iron Man said to himself. Then I’ll find out just what trouble **this mysterious Mandarin character** is causing.

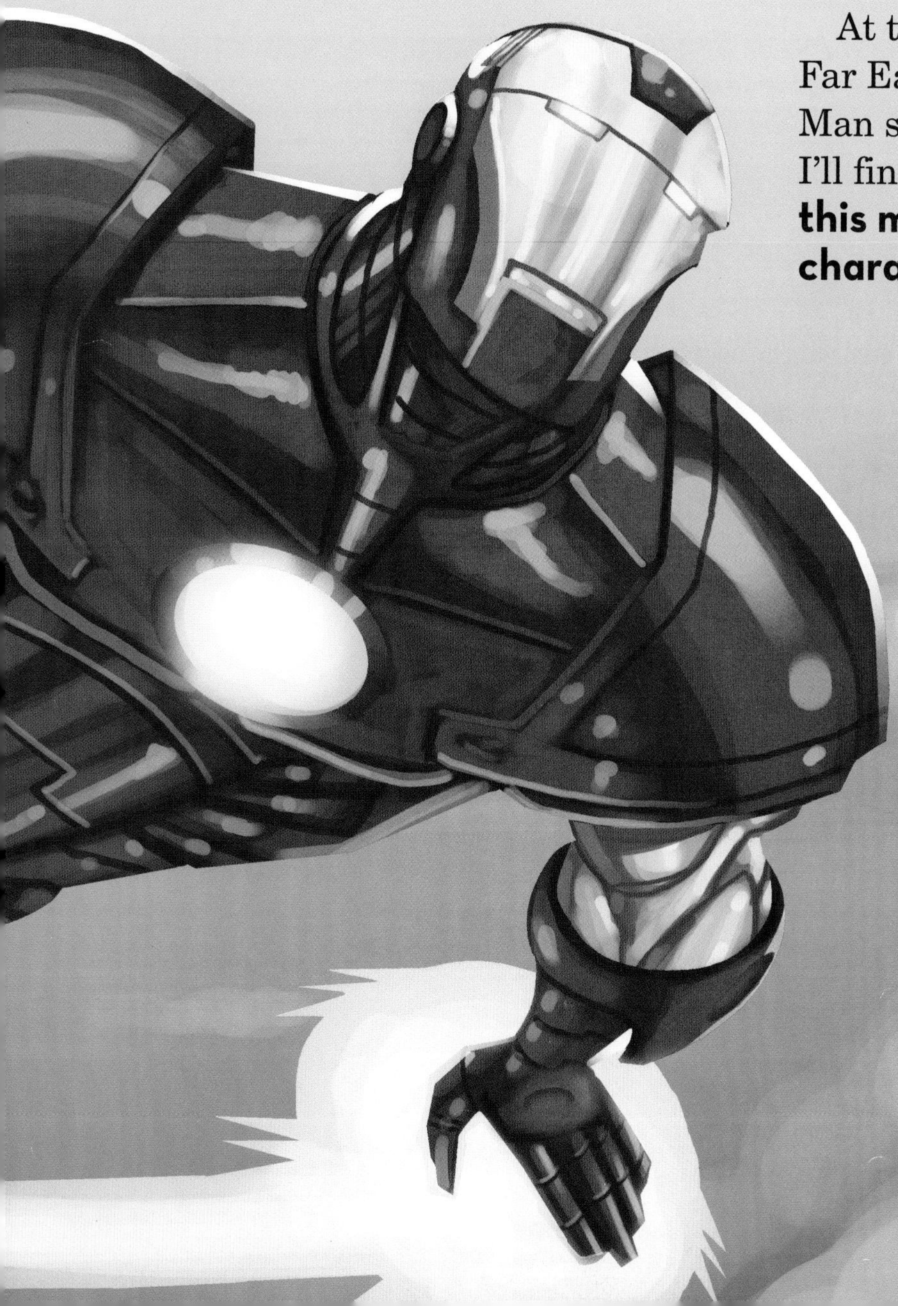

Little was known about how the Mandarin became so powerful. One day, while climbing a mountain in the Valley of Spirits, he stumbled upon a **space ship.** Inside, he found **ten superpowered rings.**

One ring could form ice blasts. Another could create huge flames! One ring gave him the ability to draw electricity and lightning from the sky. . . .

When he put them on, he realized that no one would be able to stop him!

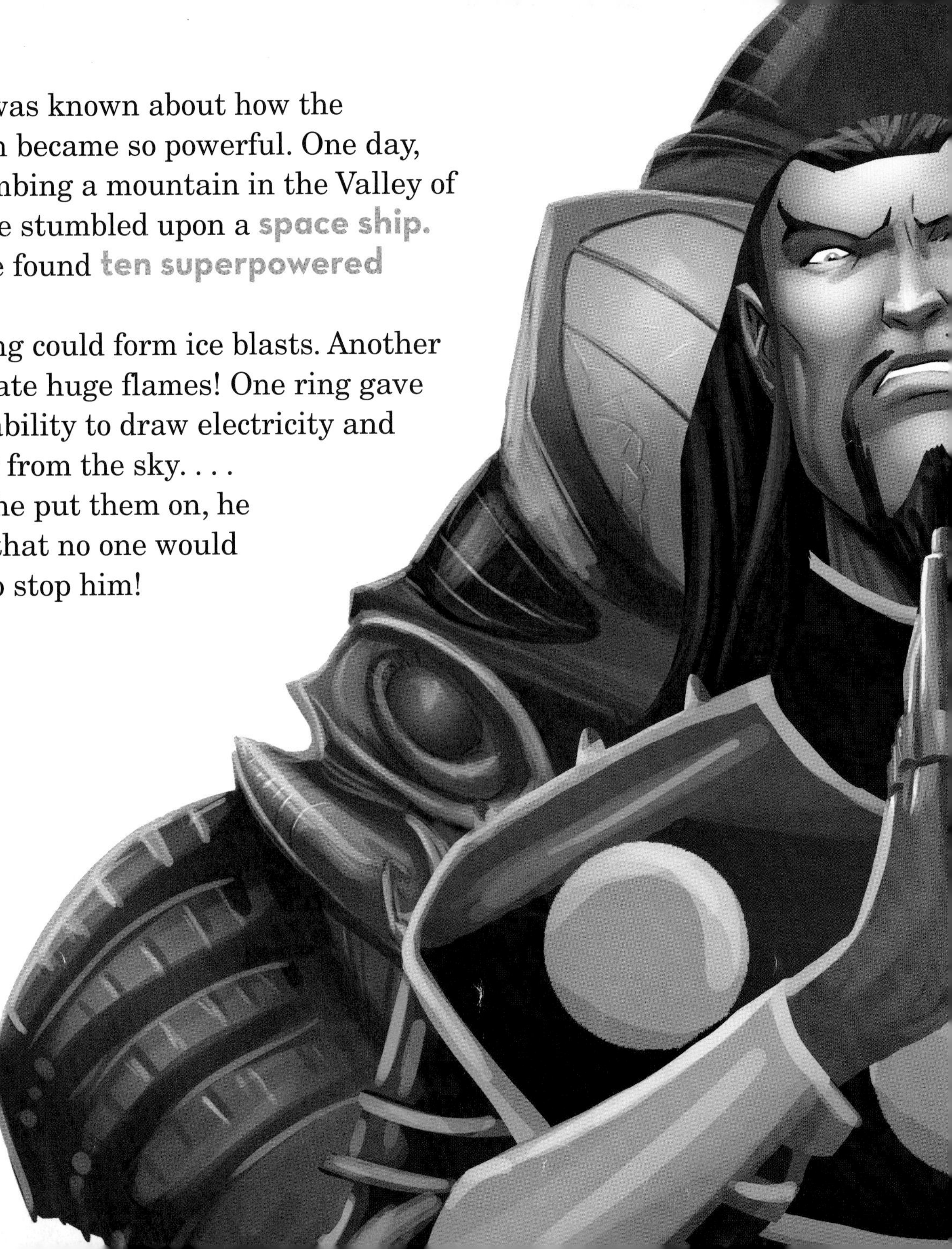

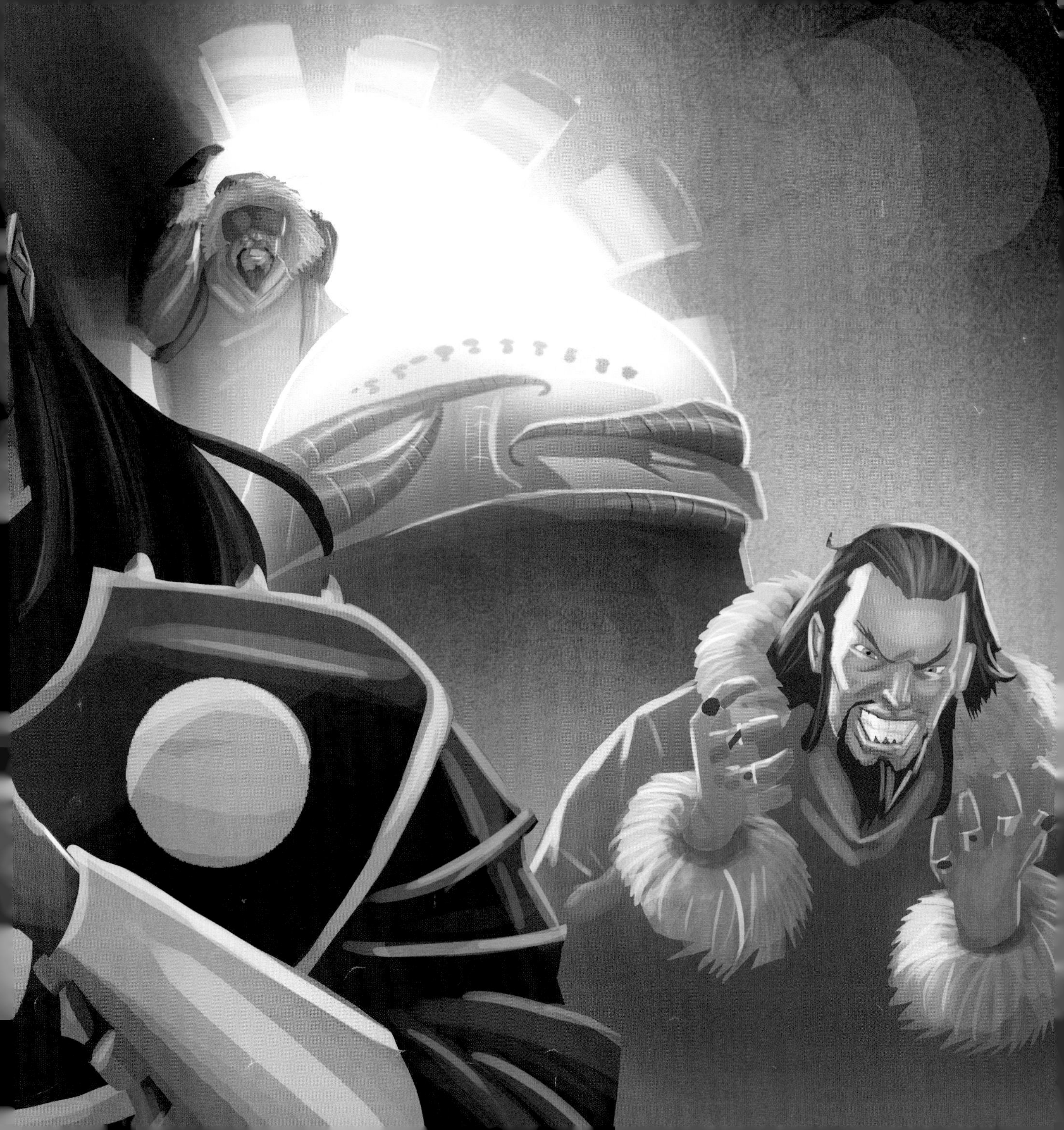

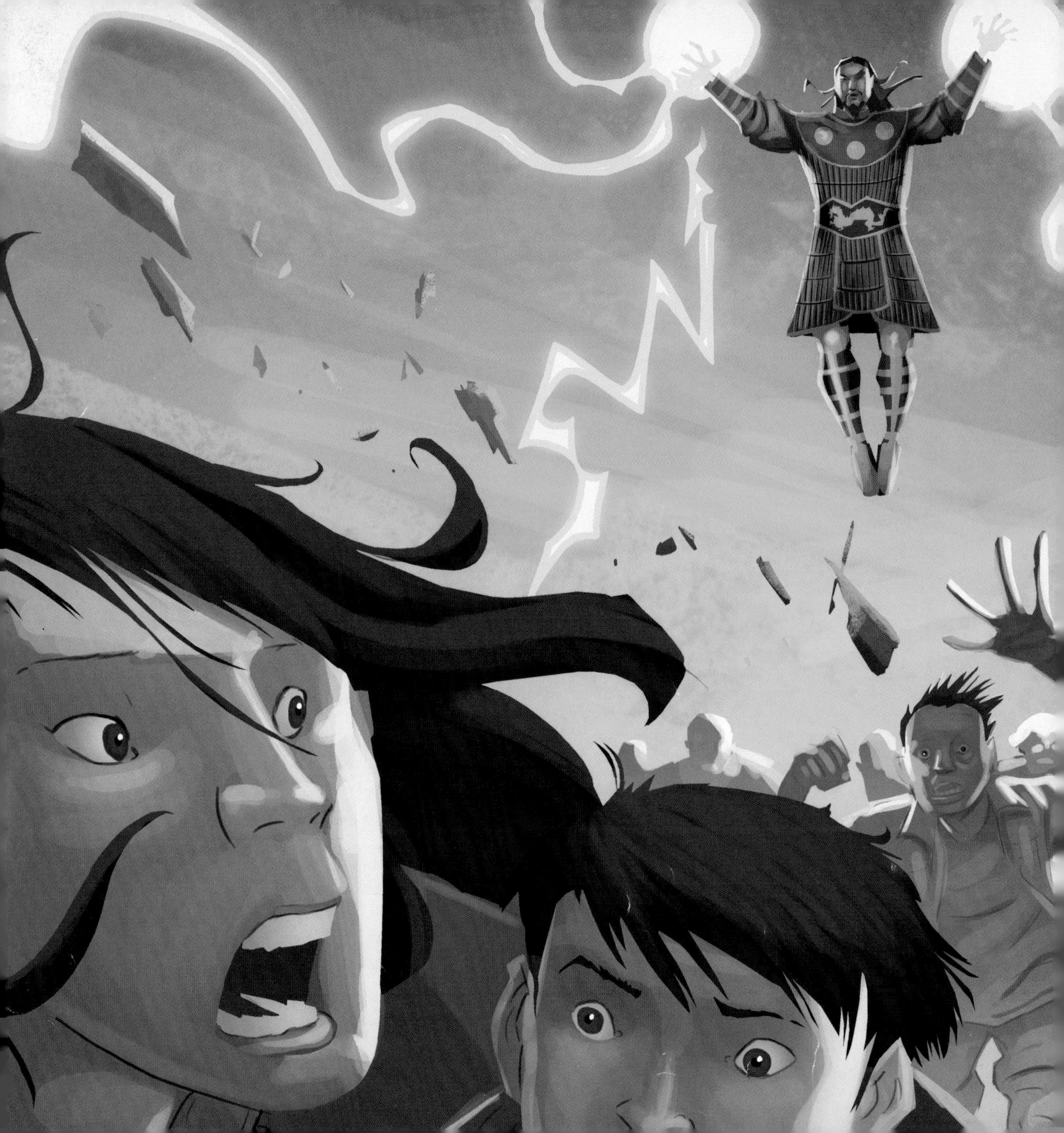

He was very, very powerful. But the Mandarin did not use his power for good. . . .

The Mandarin wanted to use his great powers to **take over the world!**

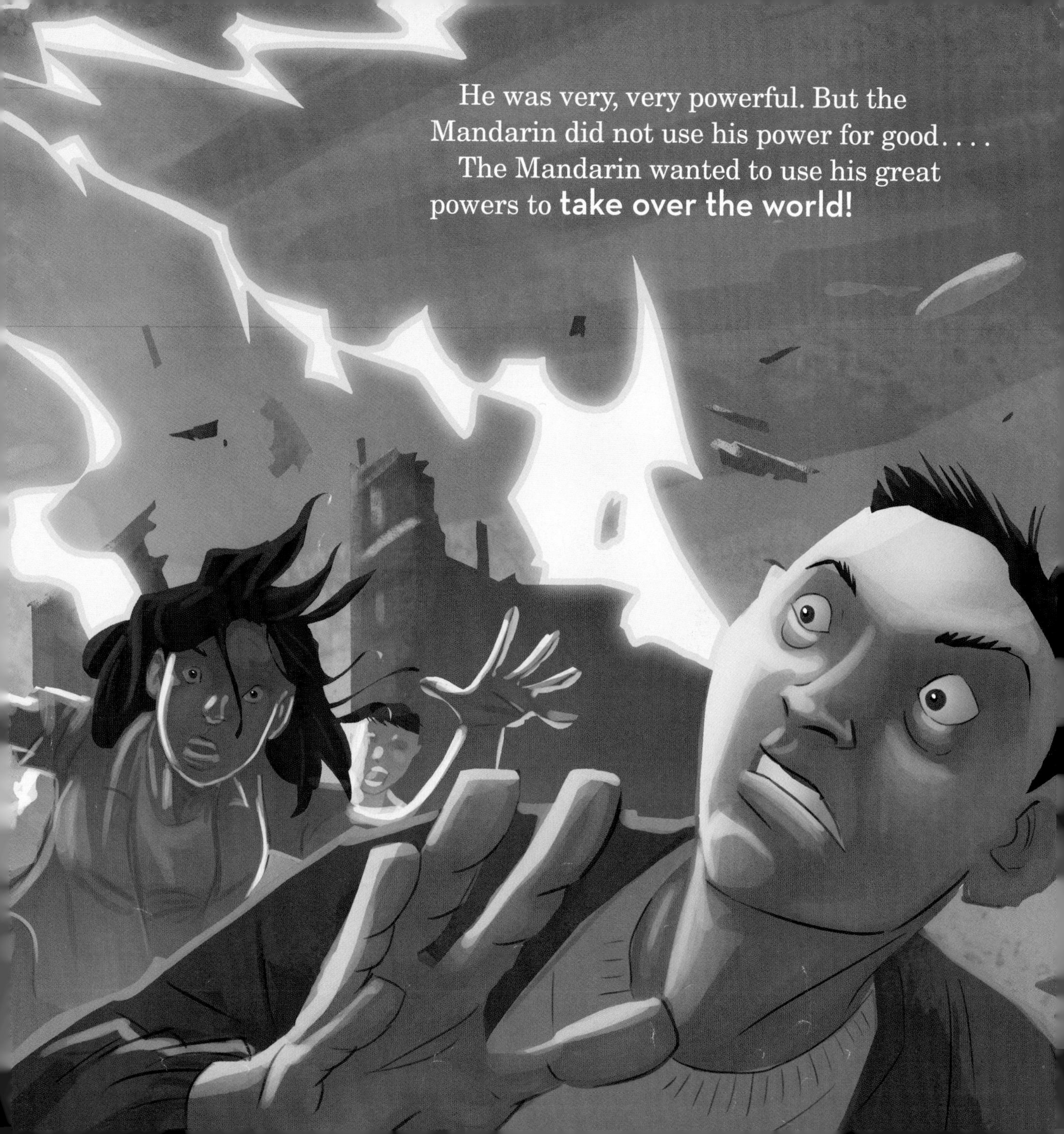

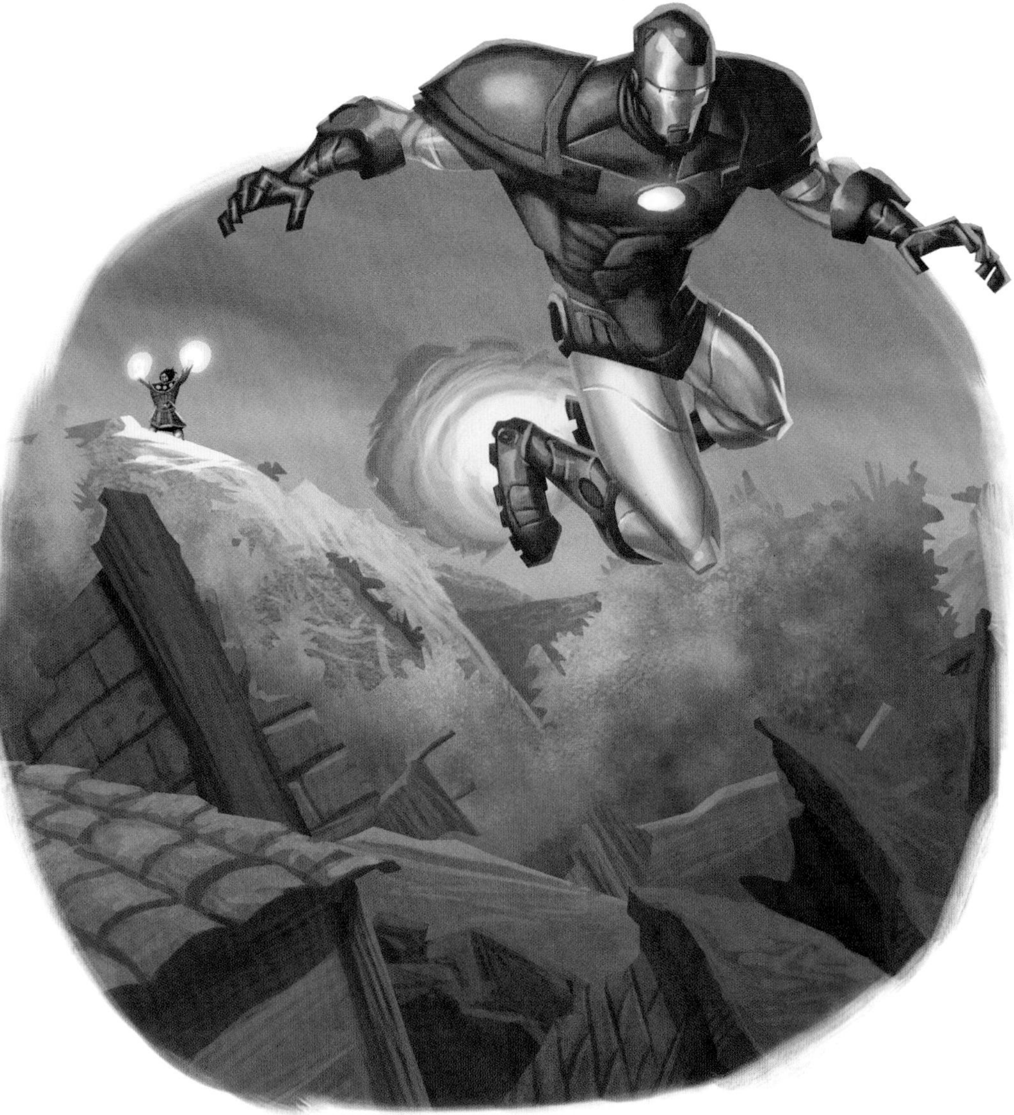

Iron Man arrived at the last place the Mandarin was seen. Just then, the armored hero was attacked!

"I see someone was sent to spy on me," the Mandarin said, walking over to the fallen hero. His rings began to glow with energy. **"You are weak, just like the others!** Nothing can stop my rings of power—not even you, Tin Man!"

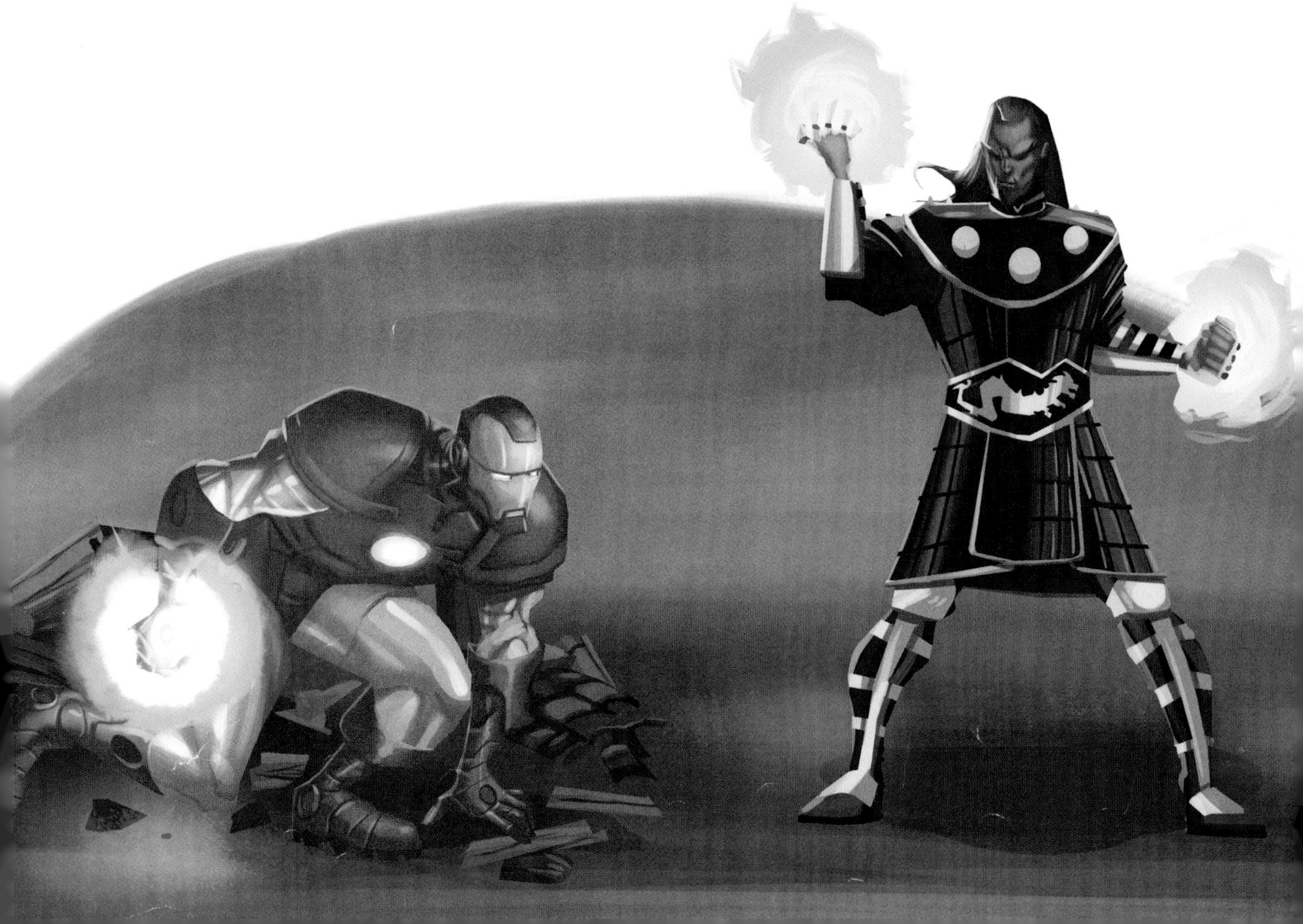

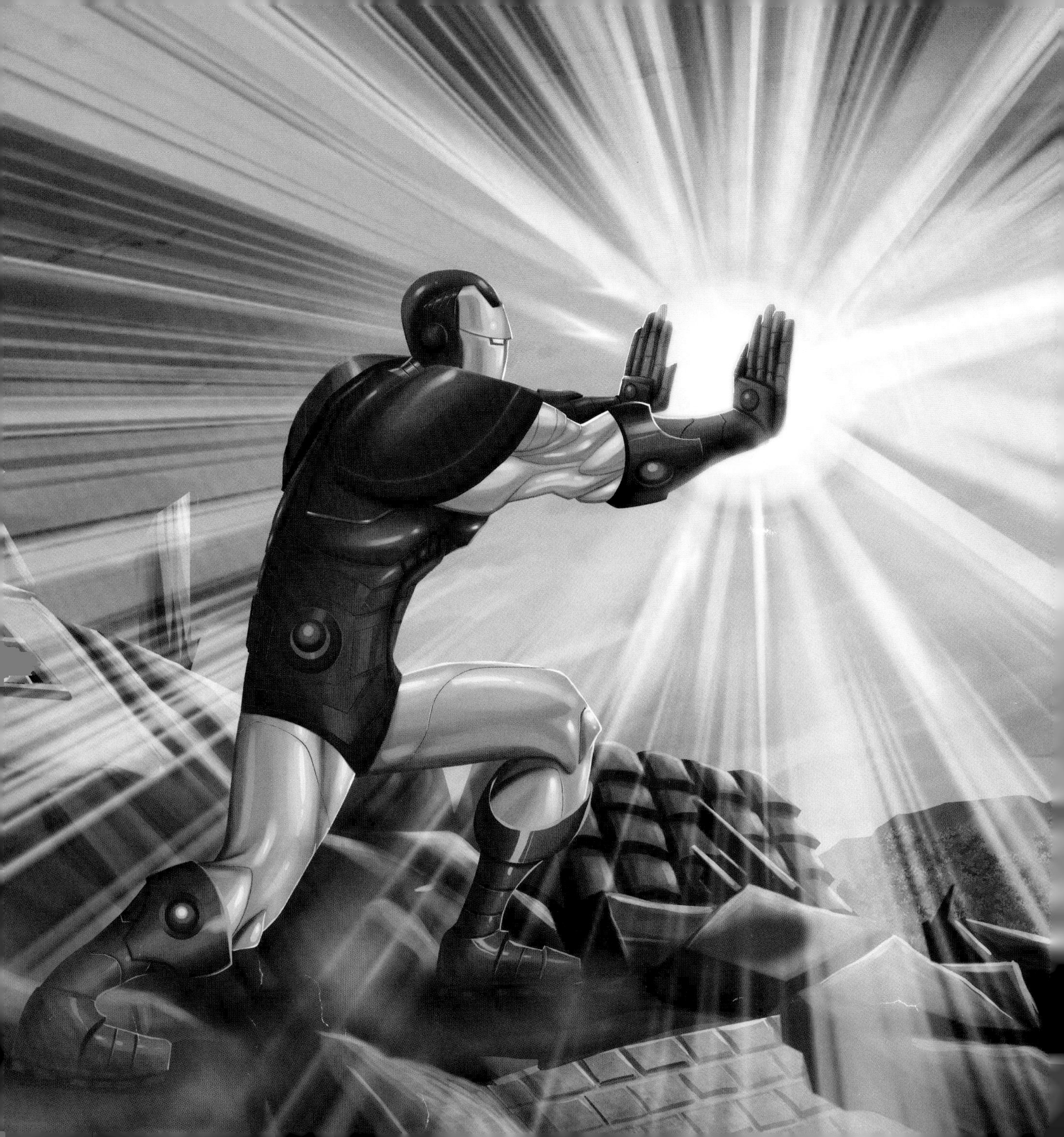

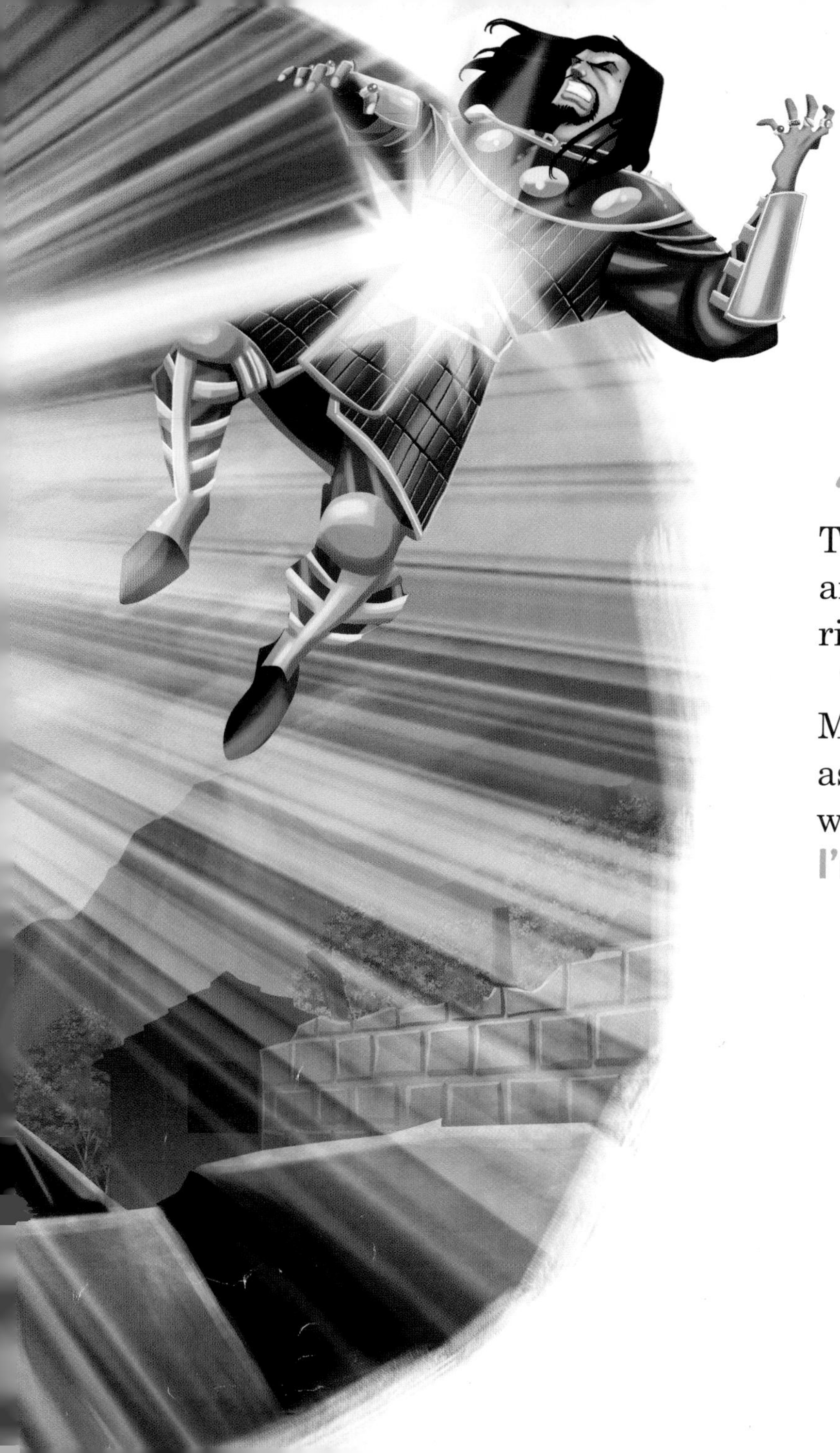

"The name's Iron Man!" Tony cried as he raised his arms and fired his repulsors right at the Super Villain!

"And you must be the Mandarin," Iron Man said as he stood. "Heard you were causing some trouble. I'm here to stop you."

"You fool!" cried the Mandarin. "I will crush you into nothing. Just like this village!"

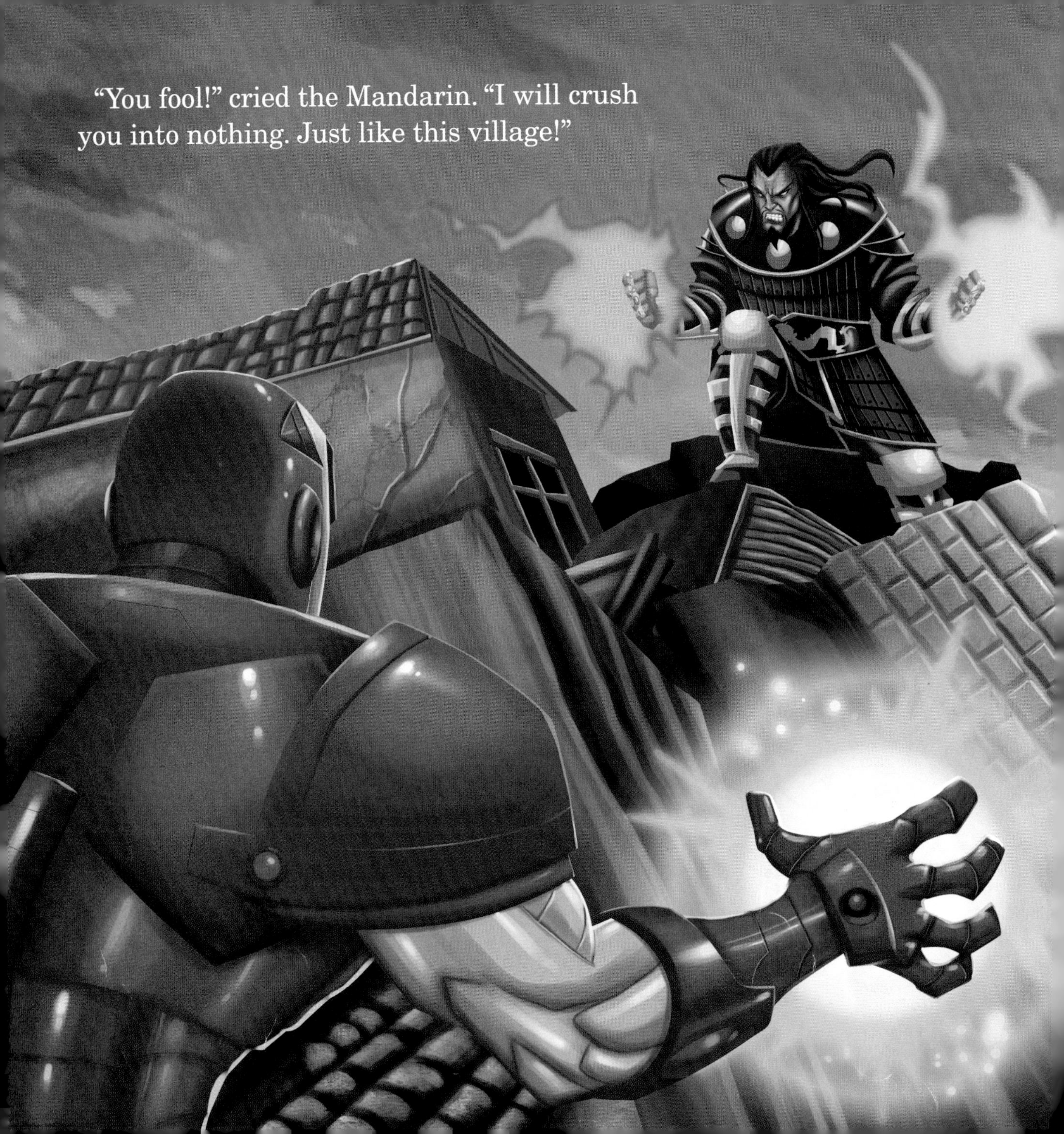

The Mandarin used a magical ring to fire a cold blast of ice that froze Iron Man!

I've got to melt this ice before he attacks! Tony said to himself. Within seconds, Iron Man burst through the ice.

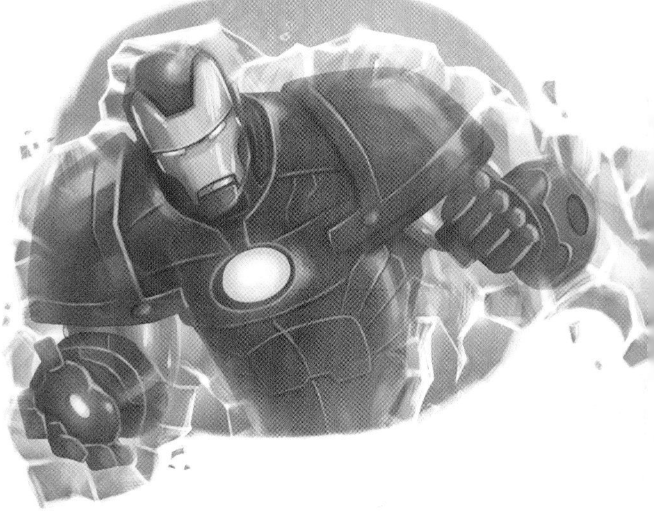

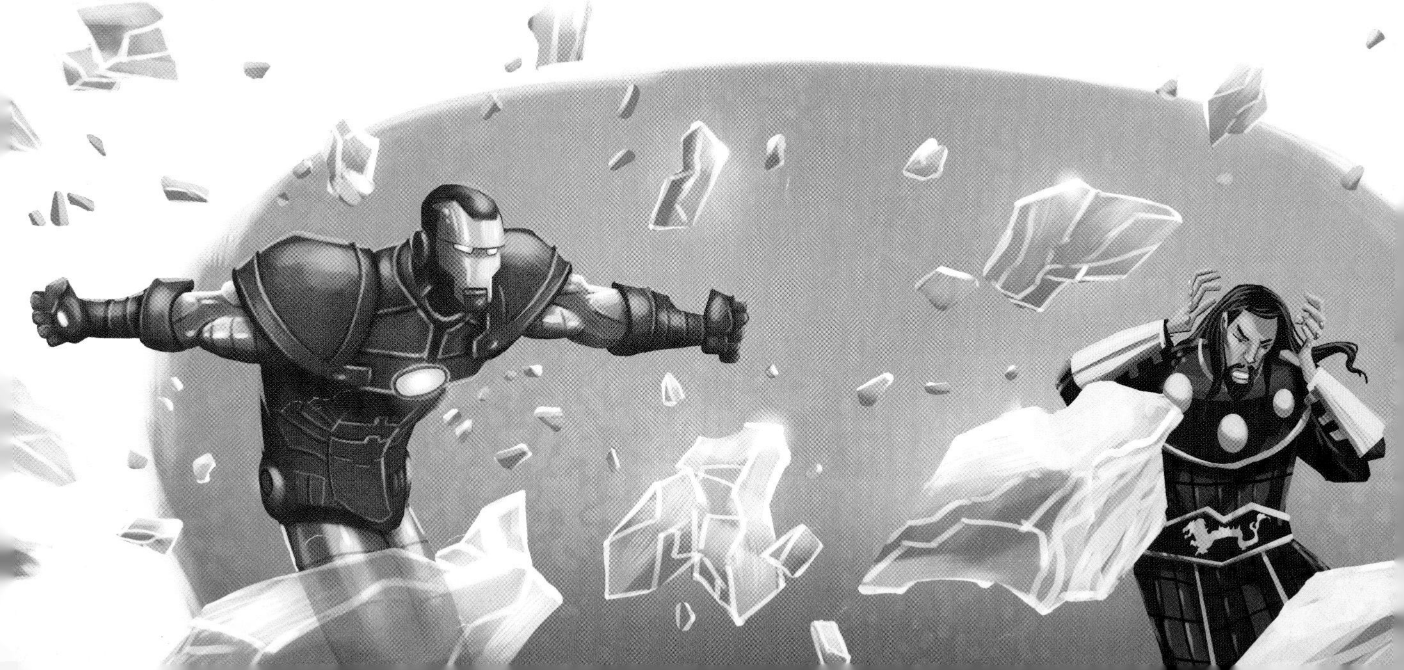

But the Mandarin had more where that came from. . . .

He used every power he had **to try to destroy Iron Man.**

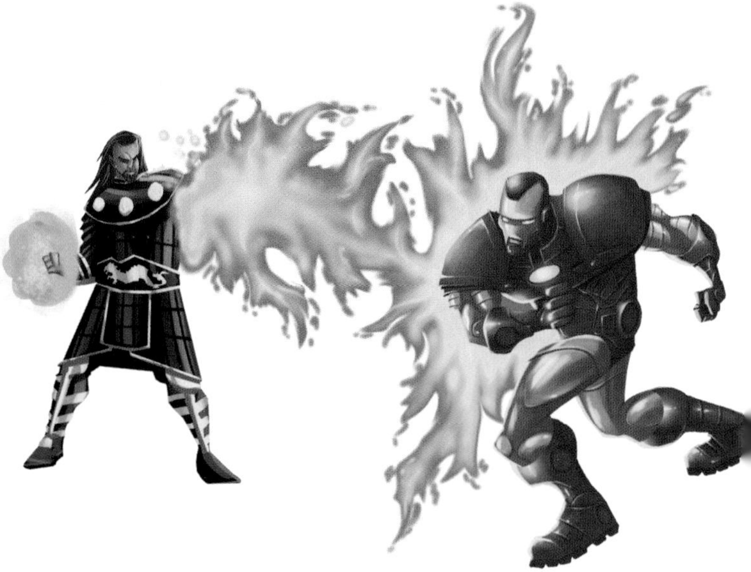

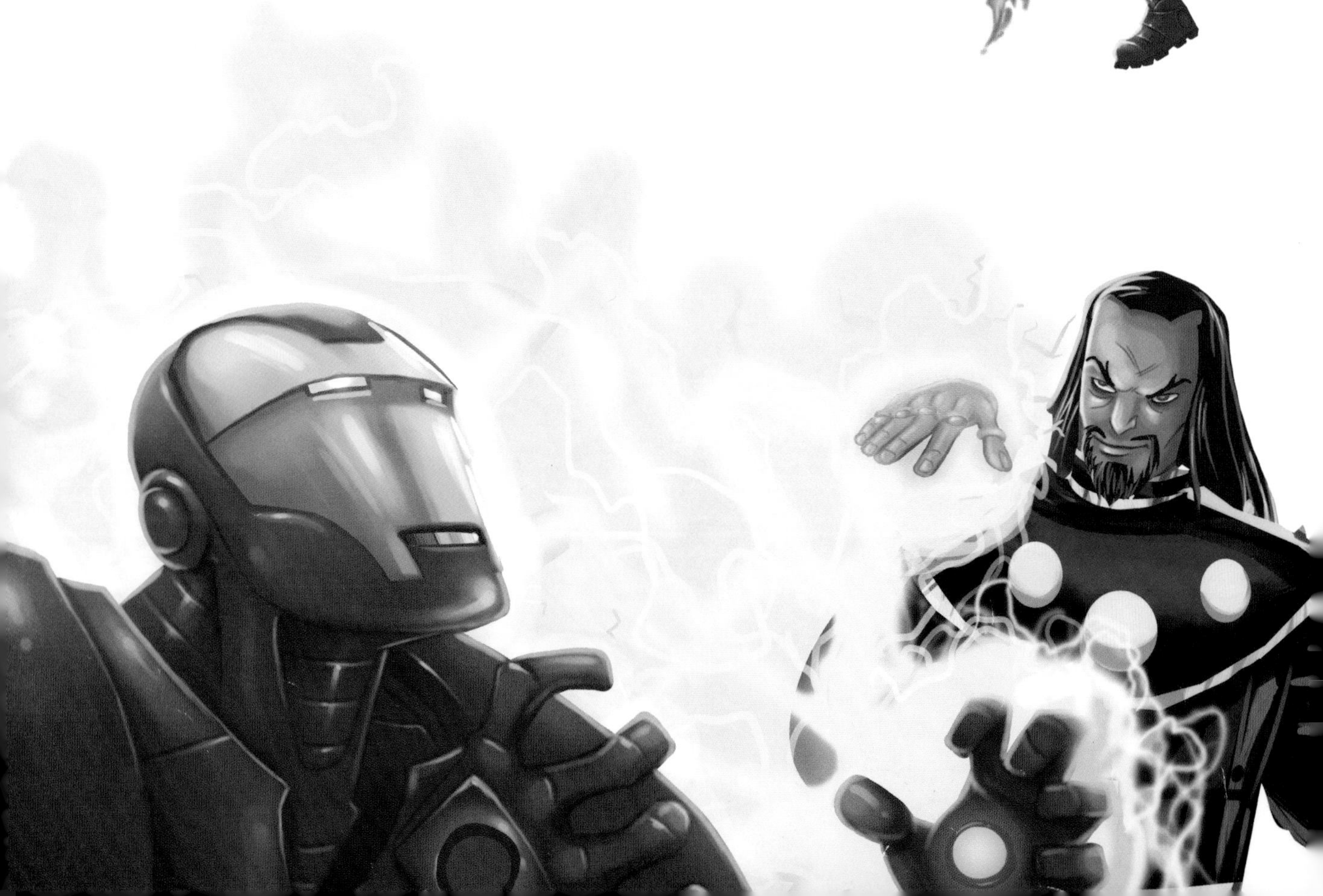

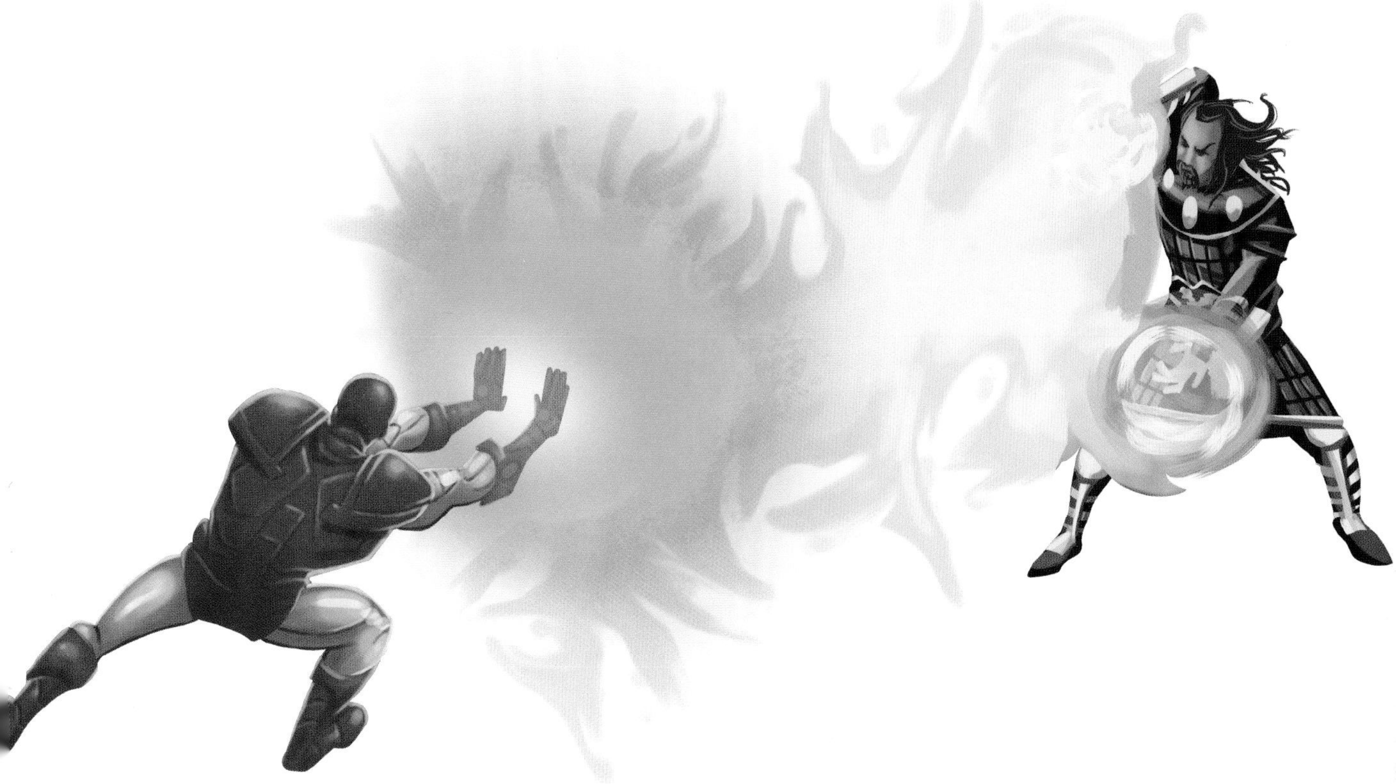

He sent **blasts of fire** hot enough to melt solid rock. . .

He shot **electric pulses** that were stronger than lightning. . .

He used the **force of the winds** to twist and turn Iron Man's armor. . .

And he fired **plasma blasts** strong enough to destroy an entire building!

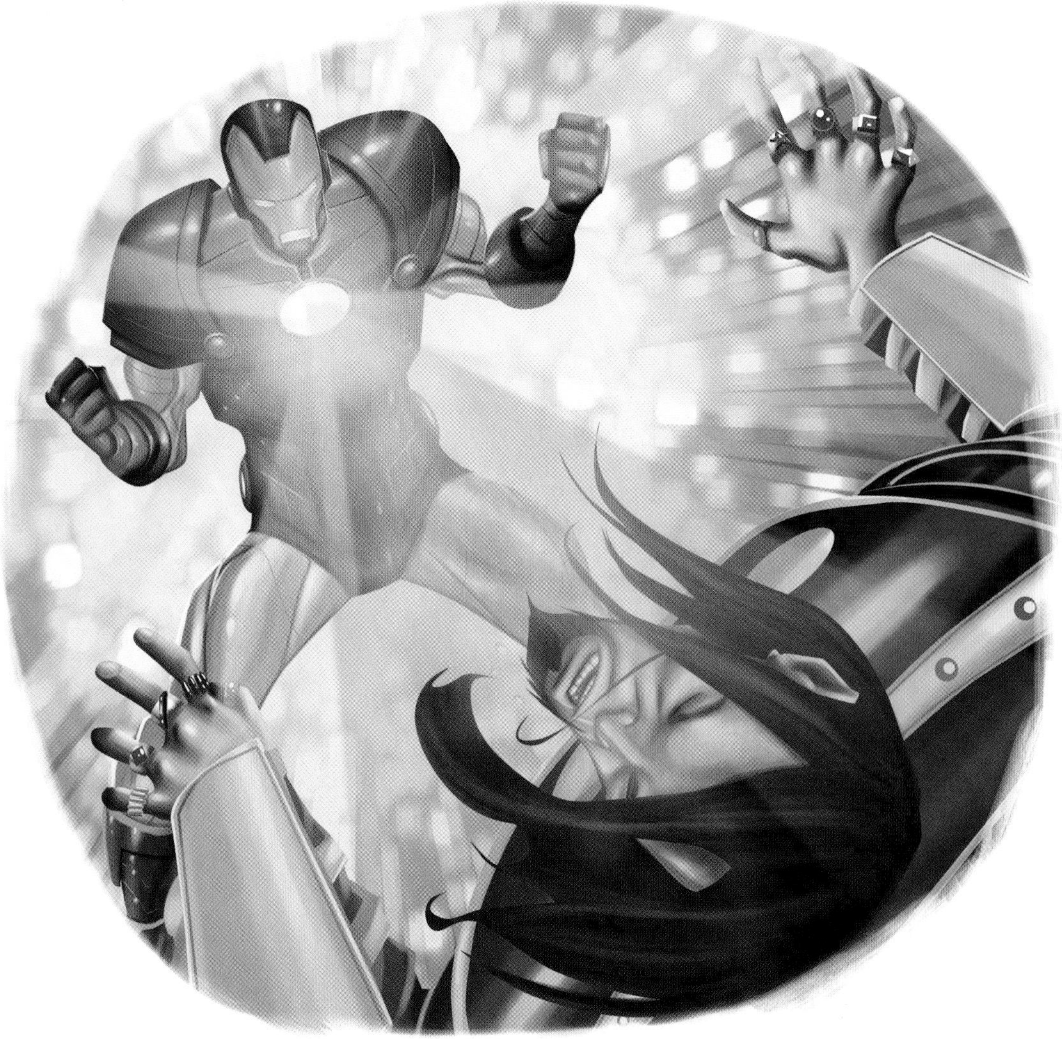

But Iron Man would not give up! Despite the Mandarin's attacks, he fired his uni-beam at the villain.

"You will not cause any more harm to innocent civilians!" Iron Man yelled.

Knowing he had to distract Iron Man long enough to escape, the Mandarin fired the remaining energy from his magical rings at the earth directly behind Iron Man, **splitting the ground in half!**

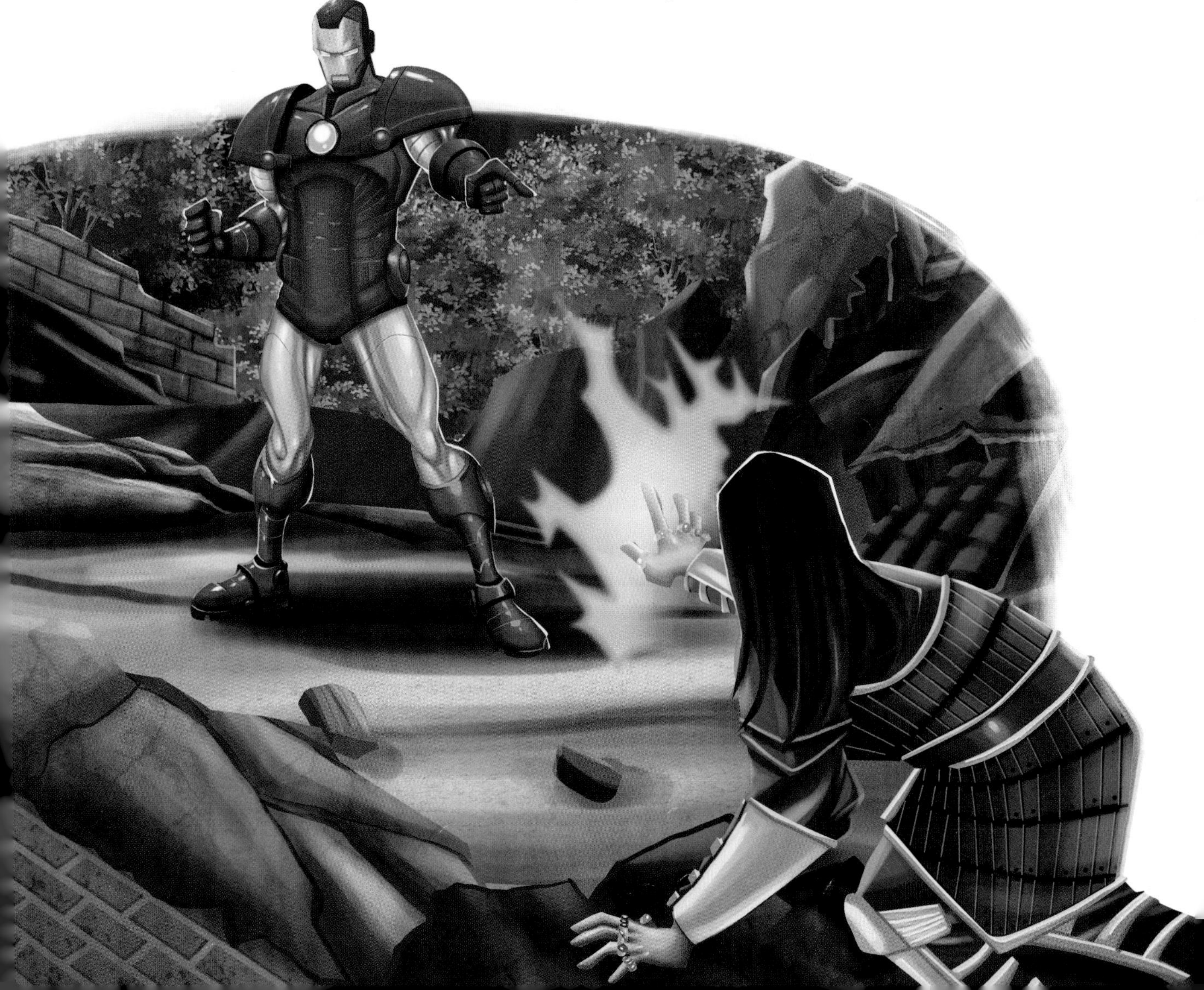

The crack in the earth began to grow. When Iron Man turned to see where it was headed, **it was too late!** A little boy standing nearby fell into the crack!

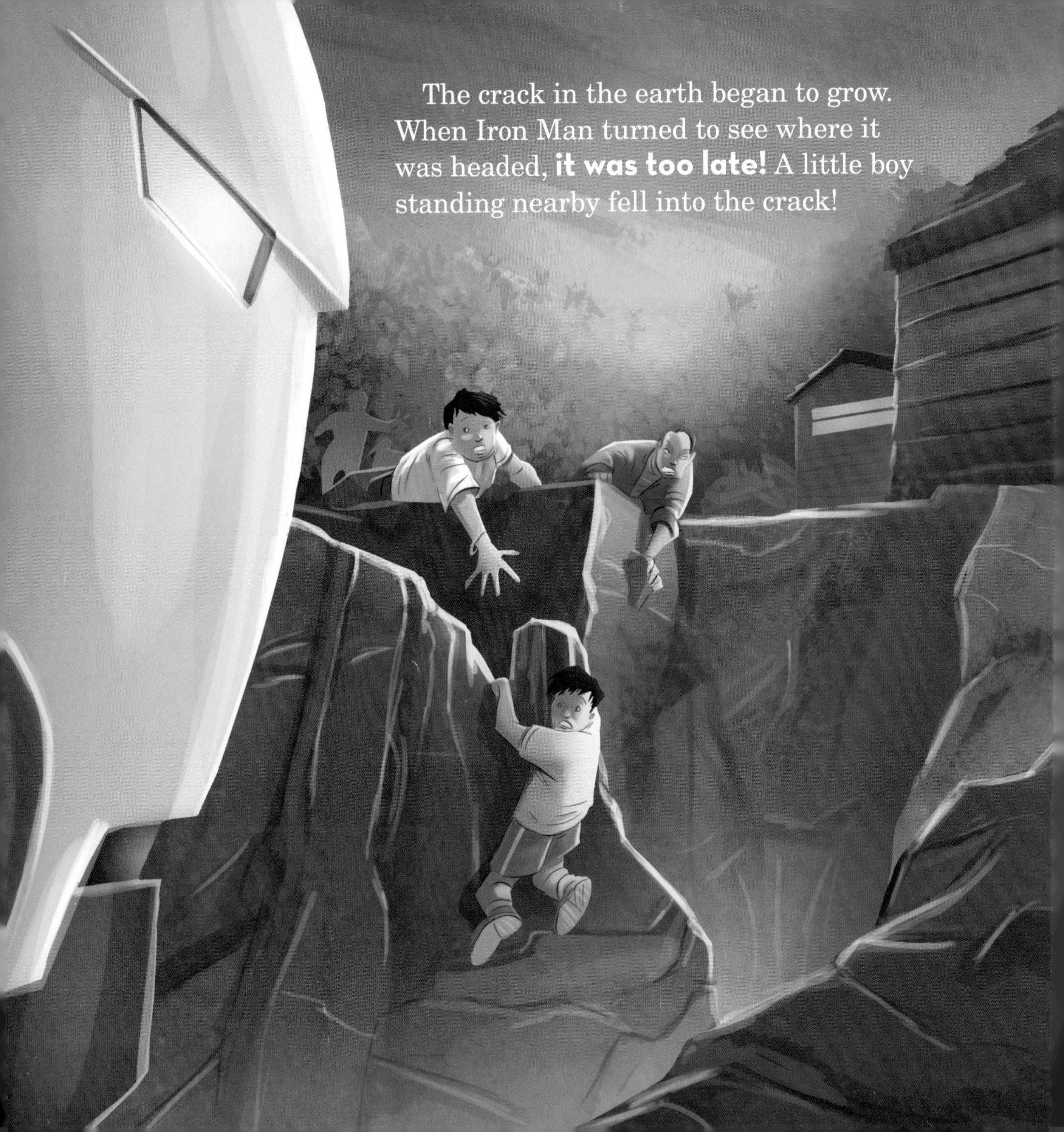

With lightning speed, Iron Man swooped down into the split earth and grabbed the young boy, carrying him safely to his family.

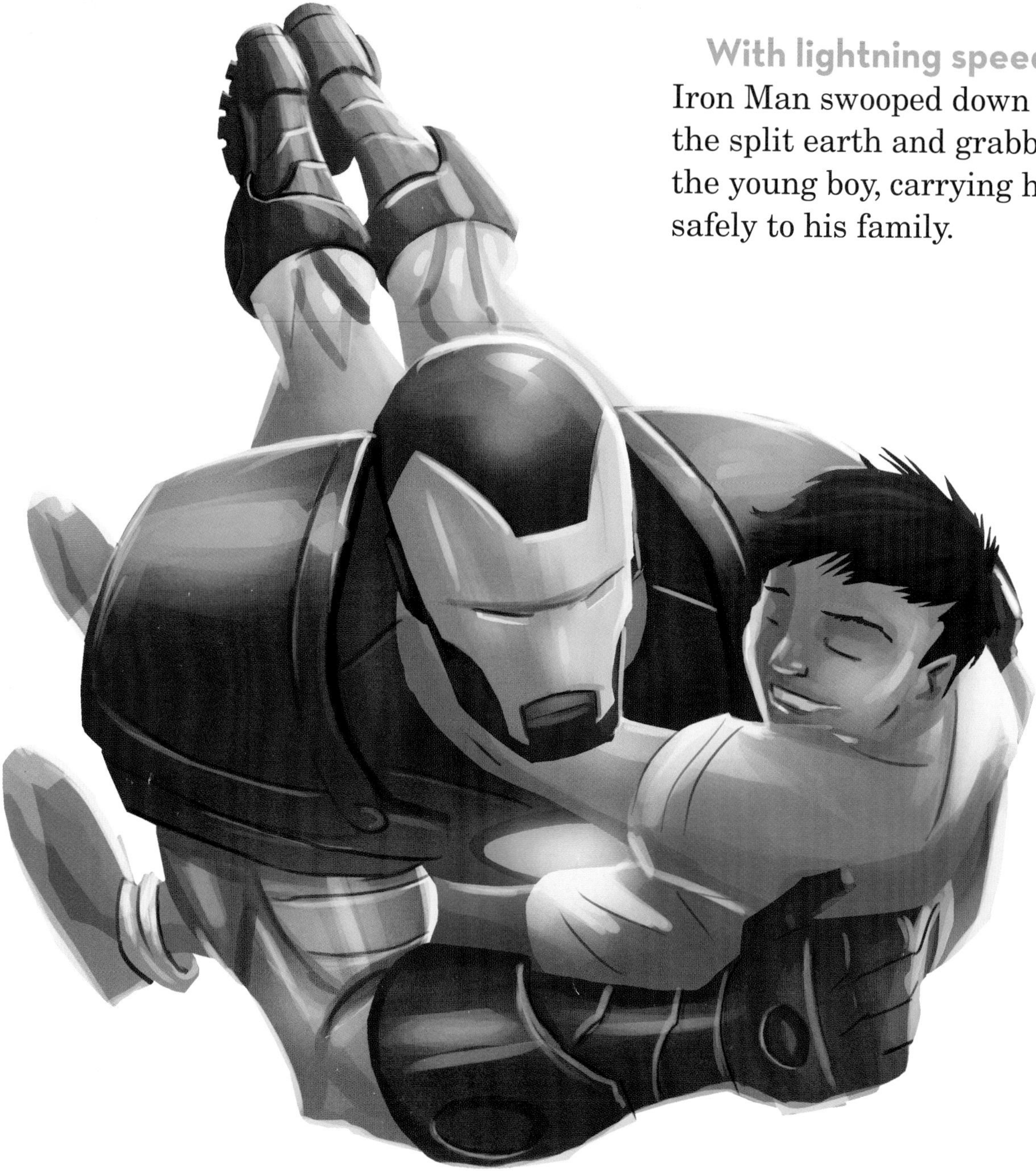

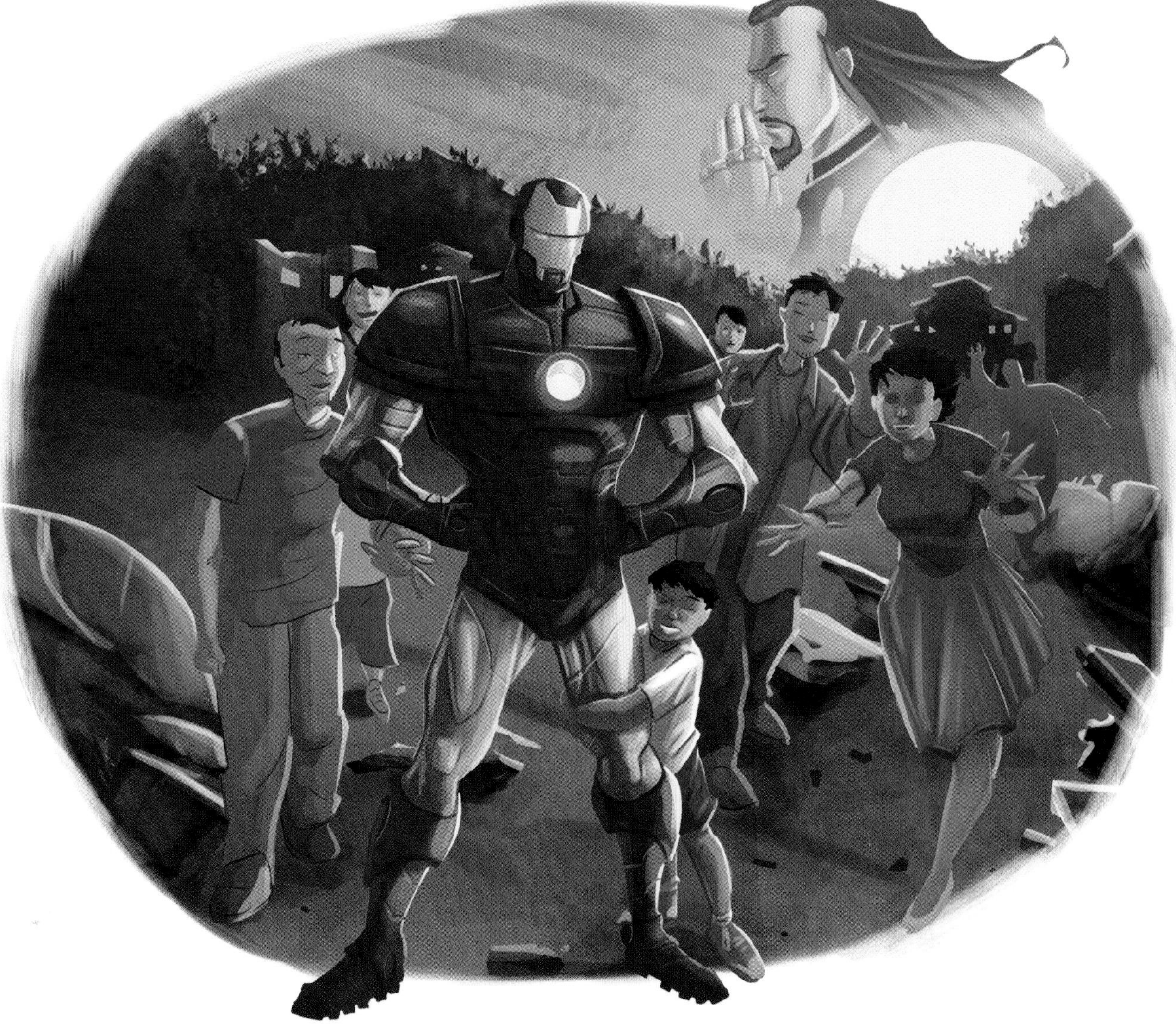

Iron Man saved the boy and the village, but the Mandarin had escaped. I have a feeling he'll be back, Iron Man said to himself. **And next time, I will be ready!**